Charles Dickens

was born in 1812. When he was 12 years old,
his father, a clerk, was imprisoned for debt, and
Charles was forced to work in a shoe-dye factory.
This experience affected him deeply, and many
of the stories and books he later wrote are
concerned with the hardships suffered by the
poor in Victorian England.

Retold by Amanda Agee
Illustrated by John Holder
Woodcuts by Jonathan Mercer

Cover illustration by Mike Jaroszko

Copyright © Ladybird Books USA 1996
Originally published in the United Kingdom by
Ladybird Books Ltd © 1994

First American edition by Ladybird Books USA
a division of Penguin USA Books Inc.
375 Hudson Street, New York, New York 10014

Printed in Great Britain
10 9 8 7 6 5 4 3 2 1
ISBN 0-7214-5677-4

Ladybird

PICTURE CLASSICS

A CHRISTMAS CAROL

by Charles Dickens

Scrooge rushed out with a wooden ruler

THE MAN WHO HATED CHRISTMAS

It was a cold, foggy Christmas Eve. Outside the office of Ebenezer Scrooge, a small boy was singing a carol:

God rest you merry gentlemen
Let nothing you dismay!

Scrooge rushed out with a wooden ruler to take a crack at the boy's head. "Away with you!" he cried, and the boy scurried off.

Ebenezer Scrooge was a cruel, mean man. The cold within his heart had frozen his features, making his eyes red and his thin lips blue. Even his eyebrows, the stubble on his chin, and the wiry hair on his head looked frosted.

He was also the most tight fisted miser in London.

5

Though his business partner, Jacob Marley, had been dead for seven years, Scrooge would not pay to remove Marley's name from the sign outside the office. It still read SCROOGE & MARLEY.

For Scrooge, Christmas Eve was a workday like any other. He busied himself at his desk, counting his money. In the next room, his clerk, Bob Cratchit, shivered in the cold.

Even in the dead of winter, Scrooge would not buy enough wood and coal for a good fire. Bob sat on a high stool, writing numbers in an account book. His fingers were so cold, he could hardly hold his pen. Since Scrooge paid Bob only fifteen shillings a week, he couldn't afford a warm overcoat. He wore the long scarf his wife had knitted him and tried to warm himself at his candle.

Suddenly, Scrooge's office door burst open and a cheerful voice cried out, "Merry Christmas, Uncle!" It was Scrooge's nephew, Fred.

Scrooge hated Christmas and everything about it.

"Bah, humbug!" he answered. "What reason have you to be merry? You're poor enough!"

His nephew laughed. "Why, Uncle, what reason have you to be miserable?" he replied. "You're rich enough!"

"If I had my way," growled Scrooge, "every idiot who goes about saying 'Merry Christmas!' would be boiled in his own pudding and buried with a stake of holly through his heart!"

"You can't mean that, Uncle," said Fred. "Come and have Christmas dinner with me and my family, and let's be friends."

Scrooge scowled at him.

"I'm going to wish you a Merry Christmas in spite of your bad temper, Uncle," said Fred. "And a Happy New Year, too!"

Bob clapped his hands with delight. Realizing he had done the wrong thing, he immediately returned to the account book on his desk.

"Another sound out of you," shouted Scrooge

angrily, "and you will celebrate Christmas by losing your job!"

Fred gave the clerk a sympathetic look and turned toward the door. Scrooge dismissed him with another "Bah, humbug!" and went back to work.

As Fred walked out of the office, two gentlemen walked in. They were collecting money for the poor.

Scrooge refused to give them a penny. "Are there no prisons?" he demanded. "Are there no workhouses? I support those with my taxes. Let the poor go there!"

"But those are terrible places," said one. "Many would rather die than go there."

"Let them die, then!" said Scrooge. "There are far too many poor people, anyway!"

The gentlemen went away, disappointed.

When the afternoon grew darker and it was time to close the office, Bob Cratchit put on his hat.

"You'll want the day off tomorrow, I suppose," Scrooge said nastily.

Scrooge refused to give the men a penny

"If it's convenient, sir," the clerk replied timidly.

"I shall have to pay you a day's wages for no work!" grumbled his employer.

"It's only once a year," said Bob.

"That's once too often," Scrooge snapped. "Be here all the earlier the next day to make up for it!"

Bob closed up the office quickly. On the way home, he stopped to slide down a frozen hill with a group of schoolboys. Then he hurried home to his family.

MARLEY'S GHOST

Scrooge ate a lonely supper in a miserable inn and read the financial papers.

Afterward, he returned to his rooms in the gloomy old house that had once belonged to Jacob Marley.

As he was putting his key in the door, he noticed something odd about the heavy brass knocker. He looked at it more closely and saw that it was . . . Marley's face! It was a hideous shade of green. Its hair moved as if a breeze were stirring it and its horrible eyes bore right into Scrooge's own. But as Scrooge stared, it became a knocker once more.

"Bah, humbug!" said Scrooge, refusing to be frightened. Yet as he entered the house and climbed the wide staircase, he had to tell himself firmly that Jacob Marley had died seven years ago.

Upstairs, everything was as usual. A saucepan of gruel rested on a small coal fire. Scrooge put on his slippers and dressing gown. He made sure to lock the door before he sat down to eat.

After a few seconds, Scrooge began to feel uncomfortable. He looked up at the tiles around the fireplace which were decorated with scenes from the Bible. But tonight, instead of displaying the faces of Cain and Abel, the Queen of Sheba, or Abraham and Isaac, they all bore the eerie aspect of Jacob Marley.

"Humbug!" scoffed Scrooge.

Then a bell high above the fireplace began to ring loudly. It was followed by a clanking noise, deep within the house, as if someone were dragging a heavy chain up from the cellar.

"Humbug!" said Scrooge again. "I won't believe it!"

As the noise grew louder, Scrooge's face whitened. Suddenly, there before him stood Marley's Ghost!

It was Marley all right, wearing his usual vest and trousers. The ghost also carried an odd chain made of cash boxes, padlocks, and metal purses around his waist. Scrooge could see right through him to the buttons on the back of his vest.

"Perhaps," stammered Scrooge, "you're the result of an upset stomach—an undigested bit of beef, or a little crumb of cheese!"

At this, the Ghost rattled its chain and gave a horrible moan.

Scrooge gripped his chair in terror. "Ghost," he begged, "why do you carry these chains?"

"I made this chain in life—link by link, and yard by yard, with every mean and miserly act I committed! You have one, too, Ebenezer Scrooge—but yours is even longer. You have had seven more years to build it."

Scrooge looked down at his waist, but saw nothing.

"I thought only about money!" wailed the Ghost. "I lost every chance to do good. Now I must carry this for eternity!"

"But you were a good businessman," said Scrooge.

"Business!" cried the Ghost. "My fellow human beings were my business. I neglected them all!"

Scrooge was silent.

"I have come to warn you," continued the Ghost, "so you can escape my fate. You will be visited by three Spirits. The first will appear as the clock strikes one."

With that, the Ghost wrapped his chain around his arm and floated out the window.

Scrooge looked outside. To his horror, the night sky was filled with hundreds of wretched ghosts all chained like Marley, moaning and wailing.

Suddenly Scrooge felt very tired. He closed the window, crawled into bed, and fell asleep.

"Ghost, why do you carry these chains?"

THE SPIRIT OF CHRISTMAS PAST

Scrooge woke with a start as the church bell tolled midnight. Would a Spirit really appear to him at one o'clock? He lay in bed, listening. At last the bell boomed out: *dong!*

The lights in his room flickered, and the curtains around his bed flew open. There before him stood a small, strange figure. It had the smooth, delicate face of a child, but the wispy, gray hair of an old man. It wore a white gown and held a sprig of holly in its hand. A bright light shone from the top of its head. Its hat was pointed, like a candle snuffer.

"Who or what are you?" cried Scrooge.

"I am the Ghost of Christmas Past," said the creature in a low, soft voice.

"Long past?" asked Scrooge.

"No," replied the Spirit. "*Your* past."

"What brings you here?" said Scrooge.

"To remind you," said the Spirit. "And to help you. Now, come!"

Still in his nightclothes, Scrooge reluctantly got out of bed. He took the hand the Spirit held out to him.

Suddenly they were in a small town in the country. Boys riding on ponies or in carts crowded the road. They were going home for Christmas, and they called out to one another merrily.

"Good heavens!" said Scrooge. "I recognize all these boys—they're my old friends from school."

The Spirit took his arm, and at once, they were in a cold, gloomy schoolroom. A sad-looking boy sat alone, reading quietly.

"That lonely boy is me!" cried Scrooge, and he began to sob.

Before his eyes, the pictures in the book that the boy was reading came to life.

"There's Robinson Crusoe with his parrot, and Man Friday running along the beach!" Scrooge exclaimed. He dried his eyes on his sleeve. "I wish—" he began.

"What?" asked the Spirit.

"A boy was singing Christmas carols outside my office today," said Scrooge. "I wish I had given him something."

The Spirit smiled thoughtfully, then waved its hand, saying, "Let's look at another Christmas."

They were in the same schoolroom. The boy was alone again, but older. The door burst open. A little girl ran in and hugged the boy. She was his sister, sent to bring him home for Christmas.

Scrooge's heart leaped when he saw her. "My little sister, Mary! She was never strong," he sighed. "She died young."

"And left one child, I believe," said the Spirit. "Your nephew, Fred."

"Yes," said Scrooge uneasily.

"There's Robinson Crusoe with his parrot!"

They left the schoolroom and found themselves in a large city. It was Christmas Eve, and the streets sparkled with lights.

They stopped at a warehouse door. "Do you know this place?" asked the Spirit.

"Know it? I was apprenticed here!" cried Scrooge excitedly.

Inside, a lively party was in full swing. Old Fezziwig, Scrooge's employer, was celebrating Christmas with his family and workers. Platters of meats, cakes, and mince pies crowded the table. A fiddler played music as laughing couples whirled around the room.

No one danced better than Fezziwig and his wife. Old Fezziwig seemed to be everywhere at once, and Mrs. Fezziwig kept up with him!

"Wonderful!" cried Scrooge, enjoying it as much as he had all those years ago. When the dance ended, he looked at the Spirit.

"Is something wrong?" asked the Spirit.

"No," said Scrooge. "I just wish I could say a word to Bob Cratchit, that's all."

The next scene made him inhale a sharp breath. Scrooge, as a young man, sat next to his sweetheart. "You care more about money than you do about me," she said, wiping tears from her eyes with one hand and returning his engagement ring with the other.

A moment later, he saw his sweetheart happily married to someone else while he sat alone and miserable in his office.

"Take me away!" Scrooge cried out to the Spirit. Suddenly he was in his own bedroom. He fell on the bed and sank into a deep sleep.

On top of the heap sat a jolly giant.

THE SPIRIT OF
CHRISTMAS PRESENT

When the clock struck again, Scrooge sat up immediately. A blaze of light shone around his bed.

He peered through the curtains and was astonished to see the change in his room. Holly, ivy, and mistletoe decorated the walls and mantle. Heaped on the floor in a magnificent display were roasted turkeys, sausages, fruits, pies, and puddings. On top of the heap sat a jolly giant, smiling warmly at him.

"Come in, man, and get to know me!" said the giant in a booming voice. "I am the Ghost of Christmas Present!"

"I know you have come to do me good," Scrooge said humbly. "Please show me what you will."

"Touch my robe," commanded the Spirit.

Scrooge did, and the next instant they were out in the street.

In front of them stood the tiny house of Scrooge's clerk, Bob Cratchit.

Inside was a merry scene. Mrs. Cratchit, dressed in a shabby gown brightened by colorful ribbons, hummed as she stirred a pot on the stove. Two Cratchit children raced around the room playing tag while the others helped their mother make the meal.

"Here come Father and Tiny Tim!" cried the children happily as Bob Cratchit came through the door with his youngest son on his shoulder. Scrooge saw that Tiny Tim had a crippled leg and needed a crutch to walk.

"Sit down and warm yourselves!" cried Mrs. Cratchit, rushing over to kiss them. Just then, two more Cratchits came tearing through the door, bringing a large goose on a tray from the butcher's.

Mrs. Cratchit stirred the gravy. Peter mashed the potatoes. Martha dished out the applesauce. Then the whole family sat down for the Christmas meal.

"Merry Christmas to us all!" said Bob, looking lovingly at his family around the table. Next to him sat Tiny Tim. He held the boy's thin little hand gently in his own.

"God bless us, every one!" added Tiny Tim.

Scrooge could see that the child was very weak. "Spirit," he whispered, "how long will the boy live?"

"I see an empty chair," replied the Spirit, "and beside it a little crutch. If these shadows do not change, Tiny Tim will not see another Christmas."

Then the Spirit looked down at Scrooge. "But why should you care? Let him die. There are too many poor people."

Hearing his own words, Scrooge was silent and ashamed.

Without a word of warning from the Spirit, the scene before them vanished. Now they stood on a dark and lonely stretch of land.

"What place is this?" asked Scrooge fearfully.

"A place where miners live," said the Spirit.

They entered a hut made of mud and stone. Inside, a family even poorer than the Cratchits sang Christmas carols.

Again the Spirit whisked Scrooge away. To his horror, they passed over a stormy sea to a place where waves crashed against the rocks. On the cliffs stood a lighthouse. Inside, Scrooge watched as two sailors joyfully wished each other a Merry Christmas.

The scene quickly changed again. Suddenly Scrooge heard a hearty laugh. He was standing in his nephew's house, where a Christmas party was taking place. The guests were playing a game in which they had to guess what Fred was thinking. They asked him questions, to which he could answer only "yes" or "no."

Yes, he was thinking of an animal—a mean and disagreeable beast! Yes, it lived in London. No, it wasn't a tiger . . . or a lion . . . or a bear! At this, Fred laughed until his face grew pink.

Scrooge laughed, too, enjoying the game.

And then one of the guests squealed, "I know who it is! It's your Uncle Scrooge!"

Scrooge's face fell. But then his nephew said merrily, "Here's a toast to Uncle Scrooge!"

The Spirit touched his elbow and Scrooge saw that the Ghost had aged. He had shrunk, and his brown hair had begun to turn gray.

"Is your life so short?" asked Scrooge.

"It ends at midnight," answered the Spirit.

Then Scrooge noticed what looked like claws poking forth from the Spirit's robe. He gasped as two ragged children with the faces of starved animals crept out.

"These are the children of the world who have no parents, and no one to make Christmas for them," the Spirit said sadly.

"Have they nowhere to go?" asked Scrooge.

"Are there no prisons?" said the Spirit, repeating Scrooge's own words. "Are there no workhouses?"

And then the clock struck again.

Scrooge looked around for the Spirit, but it was gone. Instead he saw a somber figure in a dark hood and cloak, gliding toward him like a mist over the ground. Scrooge dropped to one knee.

Here was the third, and last, of the Spirits.

These are the children of the world who have no parents

THE SPIRIT OF CHRISTMAS YET TO COME

The Spirit stood silently before him, its face hidden by the hood. Scrooge trembled.

"Are you the Spirit of the Future?" he asked. "Will you show me what will happen in years to come?"

The Spirit nodded.

"Will you not speak to me?" begged Scrooge.

The Spirit merely pointed straight ahead.

Scrooge saw that they were now in the city. Before them, wealthy businessmen stood in small groups, rattling the coins in their pockets.

Scrooge inched closer to listen to their talk.

"I don't know much about it," said a great fat merchant. "I only know that he's dead."

"Who will get all his money?" asked another, taking a large pinch of snuff.

"I don't know," said a red-faced banker with a wart on his nose. "But he didn't leave it to *me!*" They all burst into crude laughter.

"I wonder who will go to his funeral," said the heavy man. "He didn't have any friends."

Scrooge wondered who they were talking about.

The next moment, he stood with the Spirit in the poorest part of London. The Spirit pointed to a junk shop filled with oily rags and rusty nails.

Out of the murky night came a cleaning woman dressed in a filthy gown. She had a bundle of used sheets, old curtains, and rumpled clothes to sell.

"Where did you get these, then?" croaked the junk merchant, picking them over.

"The old chap I took them from won't need them again," chuckled the woman hoarsely.

"If he hadn't been such a wicked old goat, he might have had someone to look after him when he was dying," said a man in a faded black coat who had entered the shop behind her.

He threw down a pair of cuff links. "It serves him right!"

Scrooge watched as money changed hands.

"Spirit," he asked, "does no one care that this man is dead?"

The Ghost silently spread its dark robe out like a wing and drew it back to show a room. Here, a mother waited anxiously with her young children. At last her husband came in, looking ill and tired, but strangely happy.

"There is hope," he told her gently. "We have more time to pay our debt."

"Has the old man relented?" asked his wife eagerly.

"No," said the man. "He is dead."

His wife smiled, and Scrooge's heart sank. All anyone felt about this man's death was satisfaction.

"Please," he begged the Spirit. "Show me some kinder emotion connected with death."

In response, the Spirit took him to Bob Cratchit's house.

Mrs. Cratchit sat quietly sewing; her children were as still as statues around her.

Surely they are too quiet, thought Scrooge.

"Your father is late tonight," said Mrs. Cratchit.

"I think he walks slower without Tiny Tim on his shoulder," said one of her sons.

"Tiny Tim was so light to carry," said Mrs. Cratchit, with the smallest break in her voice.

Bob came in then, and his family hurried to get him dinner. He had been to the cemetery.

"It's a lovely place," he said. "I promised Tiny Tim to visit every Sunday." Then his face crumpled. "My poor little child!" he cried.

Scrooge remembered the dead old man and recoiled in fear. "Spirit," he said anxiously, "show me myself in years to come."

The Spirit took him to Scrooge's office. His furniture was there, but a strange man sat at the desk.

He looked up at the Ghost. It pointed out toward a neglected churchyard, overgrown with grass and weeds.

Gripped by terror, Scrooge followed the Ghost to the churchyard.

Now the Ghost stood among the graves, pointing down at one with its long finger.

"Before I look," cried Scrooge, "tell me, Spirit—is what you show me what *will* happen or what *may* happen?"

But the Spirit only pointed silently at the grave.

Trembling, Scrooge crept over to the headstone. With a gasp he read: EBENEZER SCROOGE.

"No, no!" he wept, clutching the Ghost's robe. "Tell me I am not that man! Tell me there is hope!"

For the first time, the Spirit's hand shook.

Scrooge fell to his knees. "Good Spirit," he said, "I am a changed man. I promise to remember the lessons that all the Spirits have taught me— Christmas Past, Christmas Present, and Christmas

"Tell me I am not that man!" wept Scrooge

Future! Please tell me I can change the writing on this stone!"

In his agony, Scrooge tried to grab the Spirit's hand. But before his eyes, the Ghost was transformed. It shrank, collapsed, and became a bedpost.

A MERRY CHRISTMAS TO THE WORLD!

Yes! It was Scrooge's own bedpost, and he was in his own room. Best of all, time lay before him to make up for the past.

He scrambled out of bed and seized his bed curtains. They were still there! They had not been torn down and sold.

Overcome with happiness, he put his clothes on inside out, upside down, any which way, laughing and crying at the same time.

"I am as light as a feather, as happy as a boy!" he shouted. "A Merry Christmas to the world!"

He heard the church bells ringing: *ding, dong.* He rushed to the window and flung it open. The fog had cleared and sunlight brightened the street.

"What day is it, my fine fellow?" he called down to a boy in the street.

"Why, Christmas Day," replied the lad.

He hadn't missed it! The Spirits had shown him their wonders all in one night.

"Do you know the butcher's shop in the next street?" Scrooge yelled down to the boy.

When the boy assured him that he did, Scrooge commanded, "Go and tell him I want the biggest turkey he's got, and I'll give you half a crown!"

As the boy scurried off, Scrooge marveled, "An intelligent boy! A remarkable boy!"

Soon the boy was back with the most splendid turkey in London.

"I'll have him take it to Bob Cratchit's," chuckled Scrooge, rubbing his hands together. "He won't know where it came from. It's twice the size of Tiny Tim!"

Scrooge put on his finest suit. As he left the house, he looked at the knocker. "A wonderful knocker!" he laughed. "What an honest expression it has!"

"I'll have him take it to Bob Cratchit's!"

On the street, he gave everyone he met a delightful smile. Then he spotted the gentlemen who had come to his office collecting for the poor.

"My good sirs! Please wait!" he called out, quickening his pace to reach them. He whispered something in one's ear. The gentleman stared at him, amazed.

"A good many back payments are included in that!" Scrooge explained happily.

Then he marched up to his nephew's house. He hesitated, and then boldly rang the bell.

"It's your Uncle Scrooge," he said humbly, when his nephew opened the door. "I have come to dinner. Will you let me in, Fred?"

"Of course I will, Uncle! Merry Christmas!" answered Fred, nearly shaking Scrooge's hand off.

It was a wonderful party, and Scrooge joined in everything—dancing, singing, and playing games.

The next morning, he was up early. Scrooge wanted to catch Bob Cratchit coming to work late.

Sure enough, Bob tried to sneak in unnoticed, twenty minutes past his usual time. The clerk took off his hat and scarf and immediately started writing, as if his life depended on it.

Scrooge scowled at him, pretending to be his old, horrible self. "What do you mean coming in at this time of day?" he snapped.

"I'm very sorry," said Bob meekly.

"I'm not going to stand for this anymore," Scrooge thundered. He gave Bob a poke. "Therefore—" he gave him another poke, almost pushing him off the chair, "I am going to give you a raise!"

Bob thought Scrooge had gone mad! He looked around for the long wooden ruler, in case he needed to defend himself.

"Merry Christmas, Bob," Scrooge said. "I'm going to look after your family and help Tiny Tim. Now build up that fire. Let's have a real blaze!"

Scrooge was better than his word. He did all that he said he would and more. To Tiny Tim, who grew

He knew how to celebrate Christmas well

up strong and healthy, he became a second father. Scrooge became as good a friend, as good a master, and as good a man as the good old city of London had ever known.

He saw no more Spirits. And ever after, it was said that Ebenezer Scrooge knew how to celebrate Christmas well.

May that be true of us all. And, as Tiny Tim once said, "God bless us, every one!"

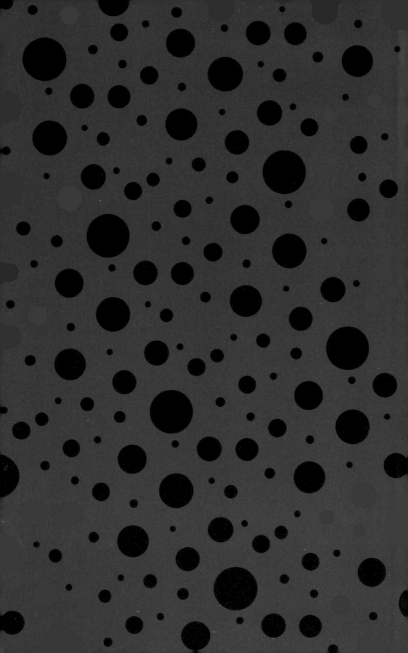